# Rachel's Roses

# Rachel's Roses

by FERIDA WOLFF

illustrated by
MARGEAUX LUCAS

HOLIDAY HOUSE • NEW YORK

Copyright © 2019 by Ferida Wolff

Illustrations © 2019 by Margeaux Lucas

All Rights Reserved

HOLIDAY HOUSE is registered in the U.S. Patent and Trademark Office.

Printed and bound in July 2019 at Maple Press, York, PA, USA.

www.holidayhouse.com

First Edition

1 3 5 7 9 10 8 6 4 2

Library of Congress Cataloging-in-Publication Data

Names: Wolff, Ferida, 1946– author. | Lucas, Margeaux, illustrator.

Title: Rachel's roses / Ferida Wolff ; illustrated by Margeaux Lucas.

Description: New York : Holiday House, 2019. | Summary: In the Lower
East Side of Manhattan during the early 1900s, third-grader Rachel's mother
boldly starts her own dressmaking business and Rachel discovers the perfect way
to set herself apart from tagalong little sister Hannah on Rosh Hashanah.

Identifiers: LCCN 2018060600 | ISBN 9780823443659 (hardback)

Subjects: | CYAC: Dressmakers—Fiction. | Sisters—Fiction. | Rosh
ha-Shanah—Fiction. | Jews—United States—Fiction. | Lower East Side
(New York, N.Y.)—History—20th century—Fiction. | New York
(N.Y.)—History—1898–1951—Fiction. | BISAC: JUVENILE FICTION /
Historical / United States / 20th Century. | JUVENILE FICTION / Religious /
Jewish. | JUVENILE FICTION / Social Issues / Prejudice & Racism.

Classification: LCC PZ7.W82124 Rac 2019 | DDC [Fic]—dc23

LC record available at https://lccn.loc.gov/2018060600

ISBN: 978-0-8234-4365-9 (hardcover)

RO455444059

With love for my mother,
Shirley Mevorach,
who helped me remember
and whom I now remember

# CONTENTS

# Rachel's Roses

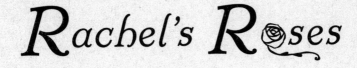

# · one ·

# HOT PEPPER

*Rachel* ran up the stoop to her apartment above Skolnik's Candy Store in the tenement building. She had been waiting all day for school to be over. She and her friends were going to have a jump rope contest, and she hoped she wouldn't have to include Hannah. Her little sister was always ruining their games.

"Hello, Bubbie," she called to her grandmother.

Bubbie was hanging a load of dripping wash on the clothesline outside the kitchen window.

"Mama said you shouldn't be standing so much because of your sore feet."

"Ah, Racheleh, Mr. Kupferman doesn't pay me to give him back wet laundry. Besides, if you twist your arm, you don't feel your toothache."

Bubbie was always saying things like that. Most of the time Rachel didn't understand what she meant. When Rachel asked her to explain, Bubbie just smiled and said, "Someday you'll know."

Rachel kissed her grandmother on the cheek, put down her schoolbooks, and grabbed the old clothesline her friends used as a jump rope.

Hannah peeked out from under the small kitchen table.

"Where are you going?" she asked.

"Downstairs. Sophie, Simcha, and Mollie are waiting for me. We're having a hot pepper contest."

"I can do hot pepper," Hannah said.

"No you can't," said Rachel. "The rope goes too fast. You'll fall and get hurt."

"I run fast. Bubbie said so."

"Running isn't the same as jumping."

"Then I'll be an ender and turn the rope."

"Take your sister, Racheleh," Bubbie said. "She's been in all day and needs some air. And see that she doesn't get lost."

Rachel didn't see how Hannah could get lost. Her sister stuck to her closer than an eraser on a pencil.

"Come on then," Rachel said.

"Wait. I have to get Bessie."

Rachel dashed out the door. Hannah snatched up her rag doll, Bessie, and hurried behind. When Rachel's friends saw Hannah, they groaned.

"Not again," said Simcha.

"Why does she always have to play with us?" said Mollie, Simcha's twin.

"Mama said I'm Rachel's 'sponsibility," said Hannah.

"*Re*sponsibility. And you don't even know what that means," said Rachel.

"I do too. It means you have to take care of me."

Rachel pointed toward the metal steps.

"Sit down, Hannah. And don't wander off."

Rachel and Simcha found a space near Phil's fruit pushcart and turned the rope while Sophie jumped.

"One-two-three-four-five-six-seven-eight," they counted, making the rope go as fast as they could. Sophie missed. She became an ender and turned the rope with Rachel. Mollie got out after only two turns.

When it was Rachel's turn, Hannah jumped in the middle of the turning rope with her and got all tangled up.

"Hannah!" scolded Rachel. "I told you to stay on the stoop. Hot pepper is too fast for you."

"It was Bessie. She doesn't know how to jump. I told her to stay on the steps but she wouldn't listen."

"Just like a sister I know," said Rachel. She pointed to the stoop. Hannah sighed and went back to sit on the steps.

They straightened out the rope and the contest was on again. Rachel figured out that if she jumped with one foot

at a time instead of both feet together, she would be less tired and could jump longer.

She was good at figuring things out. It was fun. She was the best in her class at arithmetic. She liked to understand how her world worked. She knew she could win the contest easily and be the best jumper on the block—if only Hannah wouldn't get in the way.

Rachel was having a good jump when she saw her mother hurrying up the block with a large bundle in her arms.

Her mother never came home this early. What was wrong?

Rachel missed on purpose and ran to her mother just as Hannah scrambled off the stoop.

"How come you're home now, Mama?" Rachel asked.

Mrs. Berger's eyes glowed.

"A dream, Rachel," she said. "Today I quit my job to begin a dream."

"You quit, Mama?" said Rachel.

"Quit, fired, it's all the same. What it means is that I can finally do what I've always wanted to do."

Before Rachel could ask what that was, Mrs. Berger grabbed Hannah's hand and the two of them scampered up the stoop and disappeared inside the house.

"Come on, Rachel," called Simcha. "It's my turn."

Rachel just stood there, confused. Her mother had worked for Mr. Lempkin in the tailor shop. She sewed pretty lace collars onto dresses. She made nice, even buttonholes on suits. Mr. Lempkin said he made the finest suits in New York City and Mrs. Berger made the neatest buttonholes on Orchard Street.

Rachel's mother had been lucky to have such a good job where she worked only from eight o'clock in the morning until seven o'clock at night. Many of the other mothers worked until nine or ten o'clock in the sweatshops. They spent the whole day leaning over their sewing machines until their backs hurt almost as much as Bubbie's feet. Now maybe Mama would have to work in a sweatshop too.

"Rachel," Simcha said again. "Come on."

Rachel knew her family needed her mother's wages as much as the wages her father brought home from the shoe store. Even Bubbie took in laundry—and Rachel made the deliveries. How was it possible that Mama would quit?

This was one thing Rachel couldn't figure out.

"I've got to go," she told her friends.

As Rachel ran toward home, Sophie called out, "Rachel, you forgot your rope."

Rachel kept running.

# two

# MAMA'S DREAM

"*What* did you mean about a dream, Mama?" Rachel asked as soon as she got in the door.

"Let me remove my hat, please," Mrs. Berger said.

She sounded like the regular, practical mother she usually was, not the mother who would quit her job.

Bubbie had finished with the wash and was peeling potatoes into a bowl of water at the kitchen table.

"I jumped hot pepper, Bubbie," said Hannah. "Just like Rachel."

"You did not!" scolded Rachel. "You made me miss."

"Next time I won't."

"There won't be a next time. Bubbie, why does she have to do everything I do?"

"Reasons, you're always looking for reasons. Because you're the big sister. What better reason? Now let me get back to work. These potatoes won't peel themselves."

Mama put the fat paper bundle on the table next to the

bowl. It looked like an overgrown potato Bubbie hadn't peeled yet.

Sometimes Mr. Lempkin let Mama take home leftover scraps of material that were too small to make into anything. Mama was clever. With a little cutting here and a few stitches there, she would surprise them all. Bessie was made from one of Mama's scrap bundles. But this was a very large bundle. It could make a hundred dolls.

Maybe it was the material for the new skirts Mama had promised to make them for Rosh Hashanah. Rachel usually had to wear something a neighbor or cousin had outgrown. While Mama would make it fit, it always felt wrong somehow.

Bubbie said that something new for the new year brought good luck. Rachel had a feeling they were going to need it.

Mrs. Berger untied the string and carefully unwrapped the package. Then she gently unfolded the material. It was all one piece, not the little snips of wool and cotton and lace Rachel had expected to see.

Rachel stared at the soft red plaid wool that covered the table. She couldn't believe Mr. Lempkin would give away such fancy material.

"What's this?" said Bubbie.

"This is Mrs. Golden's Rosh Hashanah dress," said Mama. "Or it will be soon. Mrs. Golden came into the store today to discuss the design for her dress with Mr. Lempkin. He showed her the pattern he had made and then she did the most extraordinary thing—she asked me what I thought of it! Can you imagine? I told her that the collar might be more fashionable if it came lower down the front and that the skirt would be more flattering if it wasn't so full at the hips.

"Mr. Lempkin said, 'Who's the tailor here?' But Mrs. Golden told him she liked my ideas better. Mr. Lempkin said if I wanted to design dresses, I would have to go somewhere else. I said, 'I'll do that, Mr. Lempkin.' He gave me my day's pay and the material Mrs. Golden had paid for and said goodbye. So now I'm Beryl Berger, dressmaker."

Bubbie looked at Mama. She opened her mouth but then didn't say anything. She turned back to the potatoes.

*Splash.* A potato plopped into the bowl. Rachel watched the water jump into the air. She figured out that four more potatoes would make the water overflow. It was easier thinking about potatoes than about what her mother was telling them.

"I'll make such beautiful dresses that all of New York will want to wear a Beryl Berger creation."

"Is that your dream, Mama?" Rachel said.

"Yes, Rachel. From the time I was a girl, younger than you, I wanted to make fancy dresses. Mrs. Golden's will be my first."

"I had a dream last night, Mama," said Hannah. "It was about a big mouse that kept running away from me. I only wanted to play with it. I chased it but it got away."

Mrs. Berger laughed.

"This is a different kind of dream, Hannah. It's a dream that you have when you are awake."

"Did you bring home material to make our skirts too?" asked Rachel.

"Oh," said Mama. "In all the excitement I forgot about the skirts. Now that I'm out of work, there is no money to buy material. I'm afraid you and your sister will have to make do with your red wool skirts from last year."

"But Mama, you promised!"

Mama wasn't listening. She was describing to Bubbie the wonderful dress she would make for Mrs. Golden.

Rachel had already told her friends about her new skirt. Now she would show up at shul for prayers on the holiday like it was any old day of the year. Mama's dream was starting to sound like a nightmare.

## · three ·

# BEING FANCY

"*Please*, Mama," said Rachel when her mother had finished talking. "Can't you do *something*? My skirt looks so old."

"When there is silk in the cupboard, no one notices the rags," said Bubbie.

"What do silk and rags have to do with anything, Bubbie?" said Rachel.

"Someday you'll know," Bubbie said. *Plop.* In went another potato.

"Maybe," said Mama, "if I'm very careful, I can save some wool to make you and Hannah something special."

"What will you make, Mama?" Rachel asked.

Mrs. Berger smiled. "You'll see," she said, but she didn't say anything else.

Rachel didn't need anything special. She just wanted a skirt that was different from Hannah's.

"Bubbie, Mama is going to make something special!" said Hannah.

"Just because my feet hurt doesn't mean I can't hear,"

said Bubbie. She began grating the potatoes on the four-sided metal grater. There would be potato kugel for supper, Rachel's favorite.

"I want to look just like Rachel, Mama."

Bubbie wiped her hands on a dish towel and pinched Hannah's cheek. "You'll be twins, like Mollie and Simcha," she said.

"I don't want to be twins, Bubbie," said Rachel.

"And why not?" asked Bubbie.

How could Rachel explain that she didn't want to wear the same clothes as Hannah? After all, she was in third grade and Hannah wasn't even in school yet. One minute they wanted her to be the big sister and the next minute they wanted her to be like baby Hannah.

"If we wear last year's skirts, at least may I get new buttons for them, Mama?" she asked. "I'll get one kind for Hannah's skirt and a different kind for mine."

"Well, I was going to use the buttons from one of your outgrown dresses," said her mother.

"Those were baby buttons, Mama. Can't I get new ones?"

"Sometimes an extra carrot in the pot makes the stew worth eating, Beryl," Bubbie said. "Especially if it's the last good stew for a while."

Rachel had no idea why Bubbie was talking about

carrots and stew when it was buttons and skirts Rachel and her mother were discussing. But she knew her grandmother was somehow on her side. She crossed her fingers for luck.

Mrs. Berger looked at Rachel, sighed, and reached into her purse. She took out a nickel and handed it to her daughter.

"This is all I can give you. Look for the sale buttons at Mr. Solomon's store."

"Oh, thank you, Mama," said Rachel.

Suddenly Mama's eyes lit up. She looked past them as if she were seeing something no one else could see. She wrapped the wool around her shoulders.

"This is how I'll walk when I have the fancy uptown ladies as my customers," she said.

She held out her arm for Rachel. Together they swept around the tiny kitchen like royalty. Hannah dashed next to Rachel.

"Me too," she said. "Can I be fancy, Mama?"

"Yes, little Hannah."

They made their way toward Bubbie.

"Come, Bubbie," said Rachel. "Be fancy with us."

"With these swollen feet?" Bubbie waved them away.

"Goodness," came a voice from the doorway. "It's a surprise parade!"

"Papa!" said Hannah.

She left the group and threw herself into his arms.

"We were being fancy, Papa."

"So I see."

"Samuel," Mrs. Berger said. "I didn't hear you come in. We were pretending to be grand ladies."

Smiling, she refolded the material and put it back in the brown paper.

"Sit, Samuel. You must be tired from standing all day in the shoe store. Supper will be ready in a little while. Rachel, set the table."

"The store was busy today with the holidays so close," Mr. Berger said as he watched the meal preparations. "I wish you could have a new pair of shoes too, Beryl."

"It doesn't matter," said Mrs. Berger. "I have something better than shoes."

Mrs. Berger told him about her new job as dressmaker.

"I know my designs will work," she said. "I just know it! After I sell a few dresses, I'll buy a secondhand sewing machine so I'll be able to work even faster."

"Hmm," said Mr. Berger. "Well, I guess we will have to be even more careful with money for a while, then. Though I'm sure you'll soon have customers knocking at our door."

Rachel felt the heat of the nickel in her hand. How much of a dream could it buy?

Mama went about cooking while Bubbie mixed the potatoes with grated onion and put the kugel into the oven. Rachel put the plates, each one different from the others, around the small wooden table. Hannah carefully laid a fork and spoon at each place.

"You *are* grand ladies," Mr. Berger said.

He got up and patted Mrs. Berger's hand.

"Especially you, Beryl."

Mrs. Berger's cheeks turned bright red.

"Mama's face is fancy now, Papa," said Hannah. "Just like the material."

Mr. Berger laughed.

"You don't miss a thing, my little Hannah," he said, and went to wash for supper.

# · four ·

# BUTTON SHOPPING

"*Mama* is letting me pick out the buttons," Rachel told her friends on the way home from school the next day. "She gave me a whole nickel to buy them from Mr. Solomon's trimmings store. I'll get buttons that are so special no one will think I look like Hannah even if we are wearing the same skirts."

"We like to wear the same clothes," Mollie and Simcha said. "We fool people all the time, sometimes even our parents."

They laughed.

"They think I'm Mollie," said Simcha.

"They think I'm Simcha," said Mollie. "Bet you can't tell us apart if we turn around."

With their backs to Rachel, in their identical long-sleeved white blouses and blue skirts, it was hard to tell them apart.

"But you're twins," said Rachel. "The same age."

"I'm older," said Simcha. "By three whole minutes."

"Big deal," said Mollie.

"That means I'm more grown-up."

"Does not. Sometimes you whine like a newborn. Even Mother says so."

"And sometimes you should stick your head in the mud."

"Now you're going to have to apologize for starting a fight because it's almost Rosh Hashanah. Father says we have to ask to be forgiven for all our misdeeds or we won't be written in the Book of Life for a good year."

"I'll apologize when you apologize for being mean to me. And maybe I won't forgive you anyway."

"You wouldn't!"

"Maybe. Maybe not."

They had come to the corner. Rachel and Sophie turned but Mollie and Simcha continued arguing down the street on their way to their parents' grocery store.

"Those two always end up fighting," said Sophie.

It was funny that Simcha wanted to be the big sister while Rachel was looking for a way not to be.

"Want to help me pick out the buttons?" Rachel asked Sophie.

"May I?"

"I'll meet you on your stoop in five minutes."

Rachel ran up the two flights of stairs to their apartment

and burst through the door. Bubbie was folding laundry. Mama was on the floor cutting out the pattern she had made to fit Mrs. Golden's measurements. It felt strange having Mama home.

Rachel dropped her schoolbooks in the corner.

"I'm going to buy the buttons today, Mama."

Mama was so busy she just nodded.

"I'm coming too," said Hannah.

"No you're not," said Rachel. "Not this time."

She reached for the jelly jar on the shelf over the coal-burning stove where she had put the nickel for safekeeping.

"Here," said Bubbie. "You'll drop this off for Sophie's mother on the way."

Bubbie wrapped the clean laundry in brown paper and tied the package with string.

"And Racheleh," said Bubbie as she patted Rachel's cheek, "get pretty ones."

"I'll get the prettiest buttons in Mr. Solomon's whole store!"

She took the package and ran back down the stairs.

Sophie was on her stoop, writing in her notebook.

"I'm almost finished," she said. "I just want to get down Mollie and Simcha's argument for my father. You never can tell when he'll be back and I don't want to forget anything."

"The book is getting full," said Rachel.

"He's been gone six months," Sophie said. "Wouldn't it be nice if he showed up for the holiday?" She scribbled a few more lines. "There. I'm finished. Now I'll run up and put the book away. It'll only take a second."

Rachel gave Sophie the laundry to take up too. She was glad that Papa was a shoe salesman in a store and not a peddler on the road all the time like Sophie's father.

"I have to buy five buttons," Rachel said when Sophie returned. "Two are for Hannah's skirt and three are for mine."

They had just arrived at Mr. Solomon's store when Izzy raced up behind them. He tugged one of Rachel's long, dark braids as he passed.

"Ouch!" she cried.

Izzy laughed and kept running down the street.

"I'll get you, Isadore Shapiro!" Rachel yelled after him.

Izzy turned around, stuck his thumbs in his ears, and wiggled his fingers. Then he disappeared around the corner.

"He is such a pest," said Sophie.

"I can't be bothered by Izzy right now." Rachel pushed open the door to Mr. Solomon's store and walked in.

Mr. Solomon was having a lace sale. The small store

was very crowded. Rachel and Sophie squeezed through the shoppers at the front tables where the lace was and went straight to the button bins at the back. Their high-button shoes scraped the worn wooden floor as they walked.

There were three boxes filled with buttons. One had button cards. Some of the cards had three buttons on them. Some had five buttons to a card. All the cards cost five cents.

Rachel picked up a five-button card. That was how many she needed for both skirts. She had just enough money for one card, but then she would have the same buttons as Hannah. She put the card back down.

She looked over at the next box. Some buttons were on a card, while others were loose in the box. There was a handmade sign that said ON SALE. Rachel hoped she could find two buttons of one kind and three of another for the same five cents. But the sale buttons were mostly plain. None of them were pretty enough for her skirt.

On the third box was a sign that said FANCY. There were no cards, just loose buttons. Rachel knew those buttons would be too expensive. She wouldn't even look.

She went back to the first box and picked up the cards, one by one, trying to find the perfect buttons.

After a while she stopped looking and sighed.

"I'll never find them, Sophie."

"How about these?" Sophie said.

She showed a card to Rachel. There were five small round buttons with colorful polka dots on them.

"They're just right for Hannah," said Rachel, "but I want something really unusual for my skirt."

Her eyes kept peeking over at the loose buttons in the FANCY box. *Maybe just a little look,* she thought.

At once, Rachel saw what she wanted: three round

glass buttons with perfect little red roses inside. The roses looked as if they had grown in there.

"Look, Sophie," she whispered as if talking out loud would make them disappear.

Sophie, who had just learned how, whistled.

"Shh," said Rachel when one of the women looked over.

She scooped the buttons out of the box and held them in the palm of her hand.

"Did you ever see anything so beautiful? I could buy these for me and get two others for Hannah. Oh, I hope they don't cost too much."

Rachel brought the three buttons to Mr. Solomon at the front counter.

"Ah, you have good taste, Rachel," Mr. Solomon said. "Those are my finest buttons. And there are only those three."

Mr. Solomon's finest buttons! Rachel swallowed hard before she asked, "How much are they, Mr. Solomon?"

"Ten cents apiece," Mr. Solomon said.

Rachel nearly stopped breathing. Ten cents apiece. She only had five cents to buy all five of the buttons she needed. Her eyes blurred with tears. She started to return the buttons to the bin.

Sophie held up the card with the polka dots.

"These other buttons are a bargain, Rachel," she said.

A bargain!

Rachel remembered how her mother always bargained at the pushcarts that lined the streets and in the stores. The merchant would say one price, her mother would offer another, lower price. The merchant would lower his price a little and her mother would raise hers a little until they both agreed.

Rachel would bargain with Mr. Solomon for the buttons.

"Ten cents apiece is too much money, Mr. Solomon," Rachel said. "I will give you fifteen cents for all three buttons."

"Fifteen cents?" said Mr. Solomon. "Why, if I sold them for fifteen cents, I would lose money. You can have them for twenty-eight cents."

"Twenty cents," said Rachel.

Mr. Solomon shook his head.

"Twenty-five and I'll throw in a button card of your choice for free."

"All right," she said.

She held out the nickel her mother had given her.

"Here is five cents on account."

"And what about the rest?" asked Mr. Solomon. "Buttons like these are in demand. I can't hold on to them forever."

Rachel didn't need forever. She only needed until the holiday, which was ten days away.

"I'll pay you by Rosh Hashanah," she said.

"It's a deal," said Mr. Solomon.

He took the nickel. Then he picked the buttons from Rachel's hand and put them into an envelope. Rachel took the card with the polka-dot buttons from Sophie and gave them to Mr. Solomon. That went into the envelope too. He put the envelope on a shelf under the counter.

"I will save the buttons until Rosh Hashanah, then. When you finish paying me, I will give them to you. Otherwise, they go back in the box."

Rachel felt very grown-up as she and Sophie left the store. She had bargained just like her mother. She would have her roses, and buttons for Hannah too!

"How will you get the rest of the money?" Sophie asked as they walked back home.

Sophie's question stopped Rachel right in the middle of the street.

"Why, I...I...I'll get a job, that's how."

When she said goodbye to Sophie, Rachel didn't hurry upstairs. Her thoughts were all jumbled. What she had done made no sense at all. She had spent her mother's money and had no idea how she would get any more. She wondered if having dreams was catching.

## · five ·

# FEELING MEAN

"*Did* you get the buttons for the skirts, Rachel?" Mama asked after supper.

"Not yet, Mama."

Bubbie raised her eyebrows.

Rachel looked away.

She wasn't lying. She hadn't gotten the buttons yet. They were in an envelope under Mr. Solomon's counter. She hoped her mother wouldn't ask for the nickel back. But Mrs. Berger began helping Bubbie wrap the laundry for the next day.

When Rachel finished her homework, she went to the bedroom she shared with Bubbie and Hannah. She reached into her drawer in the bureau and took out the small cloth purse her mother had made for her last birthday.

She dumped out the pennies she had been saving. It looked like a lot of money spread out on the bed but when she counted, there were only six pennies. That plus the nickel she'd already given Mr. Solomon came to eleven cents. It was less than half of what she needed. Where would the rest come from?

Sometimes Uncle Duvid gave her a penny for a birthday present. But her birthday came after Rosh Hashanah. Even if Uncle Duvid gave her two pennies, it would be too late.

"It's bedtime, little Hannah," Rachel heard her mother say. "Now, where is she? You'd think in an apartment this small, you could find a child."

Rachel scooped up the coins and shoved them in the drawer just before her mother came in.

"What are you doing, Rachel?" asked Mrs. Berger.

"I was just...looking at something."

"Well, since you are at the bureau already, please take out your sister's nightgown. If you help her get ready for bed, I'll have more time to sew."

Mrs. Berger was sewing Mrs. Golden's dress by hand because she didn't own a sewing machine. She sewed all day and most of the night. Rachel was surprised that being your own boss could be such hard work.

Bubbie brought Hannah into the bedroom.

"I was doing homework just like you, Rachel," said Hannah.

"You don't have homework," Rachel said.

"Yes I do. Look."

Hannah held up a scrap of brown paper with pencil squiggles on it.

"That's nothing. You're too little to do real homework."

"No I'm not. I'm this big."

Hannah measured with her hand from the top of her head to Rachel's chin.

"See? I'm almost as tall as you."

Mama and Bubbie laughed. Rachel didn't think it was a bit funny.

"Mama, she's not measuring right," said Rachel. "She's much smaller than me."

Rachel's mother sighed. "I'd better get to work," she said. "Mrs. Golden is coming in soon for a fitting."

"That's good," said Bubbie. "I notice the fish is up a whole penny this week. The sooner you get paid, the better."

Rachel looked down at the floor. How could she spend twenty-five cents on buttons when Bubbie was worried about a penny for fish?

But she knew she had to have them. They were something of her very own, something that no one had owned before, something that Hannah did not have. When people saw those special buttons, they would think Rachel was special too.

She was feeling so guilty that she said to Hannah, "I'll go to bed with you if you don't make a fuss."

Hannah let Rachel help her into her nightgown. When she was in bed, Rachel put on her own nightgown and snuggled into the bed beside her.

"Isn't this fun, Rachel?" said Hannah. "I'm going to ask Mama if we can do this every night!"

"We can't," said Rachel. "I have schoolwork to do at night."

"You can do it when you come home," said Hannah.

"I have to run errands for Bubbie after school, Hannah, and sometimes I play with my friends."

"Then I'll run errands too, and I'll do schoolwork and play with your friends. Then we'll go to sleep together."

"My friends don't want you to play with us and neither do I. You're still a baby."

"I am not a baby," said Hannah.

She turned over with her back toward Rachel. When Rachel tried to tuck her in, Hannah shrugged off the blanket.

Sometimes Rachel wished she didn't have a sister. A sister could make you feel angry and mean at the same time.

She wondered how Simcha and Mollie could stand each other. Then she remembered how many fights they had. Maybe they didn't like having a sister any better than she did.

Bubbie shuffled into the room.

"Is something wrong, Racheleh?" she whispered so as not to disturb Hannah. But Hannah was already sleeping.

"Bubbie, why do I have to be responsible for Hannah just because I'm older?"

"The first wave in the sea shows the others the way," Bubbie said.

"What does that mean, Bubbie? And please don't tell me that I'll know someday. I want to know now."

"Did I ever tell you how your great-uncle Harry came to this country?"

"No."

"Ah. Well. I was the oldest of ten children. Harry was the next oldest and a boy. The family decided he should go to America. But Harry was afraid. He didn't know anyone in America who could help him. He wouldn't have a job. How would he live? While they argued about him going, I got a job watching the butcher's baby and saved enough money for a ticket and came by myself. In America, I worked in a grocery store and sent every penny I could back home. Now Harry knew someone in America so he wasn't afraid. He bought a ticket and came to America too."

"So you were the first wave, Bubbie?" said Rachel.

Bubbie smiled.

"Am I a wave for Hannah?"

"Could be," Bubbie said.

"What if I don't want to be a wave, Bubbie?"

"Does the sun choose to be the sun or the moon choose to be the moon? It's just something that is. You came first and Hannah will always follow." Bubbie yawned. "Another day over. Now it's time for us all to get some sleep."

Bubbie kissed the tops of their heads as she did every night. Hannah squirmed in her sleep but didn't wake up. In the darkness, Rachel could hear Bubbie moving around. Then the springs in Bubbie's bed squeaked.

The household was beginning to settle down. Rachel heard her father get into the bed in the front room. She listened to the tired breathing of her mother as she worked by the dim gaslight in the kitchen.

Rachel thought about being a wave in the sea. She had been to Coney Island so she knew about the waves and how each one was different. One might be small and gentle and the next so fierce that it knocked you down, but they all came to the shore, one after the other.

Bubbie started to snore. The low, even sound soothed Rachel. Slowly the stillness of the house wrapped around her and she drifted off to sleep.

## · six ·

# GETTING A JOB

"*Let's* play jacks," said Simcha on the way home from school the next day. "I've been practicing. I got all the way to sixies yesterday."

"I have to help my mother," said Sophie. "A new boarder just arrived."

"Another one? Your house has too many people in it," Mollie said.

"It doesn't have enough," said Sophie. "My father isn't there."

"He'll come back soon, Sophie," Rachel said.

Sophie shrugged.

"How about you, Rachel?" Simcha asked. "Can you play?"

"No. I have...something to do."

"I'll play jacks with you, Simcha," said Mollie. "And I'll beat you, I bet."

"No you won't."

"I can do eightsies."

"Not all the time."

"Uh-huh. I've been practicing too."

They went home arguing as usual.

"I have to find a job," Rachel told Sophie as they walked on. "To pay for you-know-what."

"Good luck."

After stopping at home, Rachel asked at the egg store, the grocer, and the bakery if they needed delivery help. No one did.

She stopped to talk to Phil at the fruit cart.

"We don't deliver, Rachel," said Phil.

Rachel hung her head. She looked so sad that Phil reached into his cart. "Here," he said. "This will help you feel better." He gave her a pear that was too brown to sell.

Rachel was sitting between the pushcarts eating the pear when Izzy came by with his shoeshine box.

"You'd better not pull my braids," warned Rachel.

"Why would I do that?" Izzy teased.

But instead of pulling her hair, he scrunched down beside her.

"You look worried," he said.

"I need to earn some money but no one will hire me."

"Why do you need a job?"

Rachel was about to tell him about the buttons but then thought it might sound silly. How could something

as little as buttons be so important? She only knew they were.

"It's a surprise for my mother for Rosh Hashanah."

"I shine shoes before and after school," said Izzy. "Maybe you can shine shoes too."

"I don't have enough money to buy a brush and polish."

"Maybe you could sell one of your braids," said Izzy.

"Never!" said Rachel. She knew some ladies sold their hair to wigmakers, but she couldn't imagine doing that.

"Or you could watch my little brother so I don't have to."

Rachel shook her head. She had enough trouble watching Hannah, and Izzy's little brother, Jacob, was more than a handful. Izzy was always running after him.

"Well, then I've run out of ideas. Sorry." Izzy got up and continued down the street.

Rachel threw the pear core into the basket at the end of Phil's cart. Soon her mother would ask for the buttons again, buttons Rachel didn't have. Never had the holiday seemed to come so quickly.

Rachel went upstairs wondering how she would ever get those buttons. Maybe Bubbie could help.

When Rachel entered, Bubbie was busy in the kitchen with the laundry bundles.

"Here, Racheleh. Bring this over to Mr. Bloom at the drugstore. It's his shirts. I promised them for today."

This was no time to ask Bubbie anything. Rachel started for the door, the brown bundle cradled in her arms like a baby.

"Take me!" yelled Hannah.

"Do I have to, Bubbie? She's so slow."

"Speed is only good for catching flies," said Bubbie.

"Let's go," Rachel told Hannah.

"I made my own braids today, Rachel," Hannah said as they walked to the drugstore at the far end of the street.

Rachel looked at the two tangles of hair hanging down Hannah's back.

"They're a mess," she said.

"Bubbie said they were nice."

In the drugstore, Rachel gave Mr. Bloom his shirts. He was just thanking her when the telephone rang.

Mr. Bloom had the only telephone on the block. It was a big wooden box that hung on the wall. Everyone got calls there. A telephone call meant news. Sometimes it was good. Sometimes it was sad. It was always exciting.

He went to answer the phone's jangling cry.

"It's for Mrs. Miller," he said. "Quick, Rachel, run and tell her she has a call."

Rachel ran out of the store with Hannah right behind her.

"Don't forget me, Rachel!" her sister panted.

"Well, hurry up."

They raced across the street to Mrs. Miller's. Rachel sped up the first flight of stairs. Hannah tried to keep up but her little legs couldn't go as fast.

"Wait, Rachel!" she called.

Rachel reached back for Hannah's hand. She pulled her up the rest of the stairs.

When they got to Mrs. Miller's apartment, Rachel banged on the door.

"Mrs. Miller, you have a telephone call!"

Mrs. Miller quickly opened the door to the two breathless girls.

"A telephone call!" she said.

Mrs. Miller grabbed her purse, took out a penny, and pressed it into Rachel's hand. Then she hurried down the stairs. Rachel stared at the penny. She hadn't known that people gave pennies for telephone messages. If she could deliver telephone messages every day for Mr. Bloom, she could get lots of pennies. Then she could pay Mr. Solomon for the buttons!

"Come on, Rachel," said Hannah. "Let's see who it is."

Hannah held on to Rachel's hand and they both rushed down the stairs after Mrs. Miller.

In the drugstore, Mrs. Miller shushed everyone so she could hear better.

"It's my brother," she announced. "His wife just had another boy."

*"Mazel tov!"* said Mr. Bloom.

Everyone in the store sent Mrs. Miller's brother congratulations.

While Mrs. Miller talked into the phone, Rachel figured out if she gave three messages a day, by the end of the week she would have fifteen pennies. With the six cents she had saved and with Mama's nickel she would have twenty-six cents, one penny more than she needed for the buttons. She could give her mother the extra penny to help with her dream.

She carefully put the penny into her clean white handkerchief and tucked the handkerchief into her skirt pocket. She needed two more messages today. She pushed her sister toward the door.

"Go home, Hannah," she said.

"Come with me," said Hannah.

"I can't. I have something to do."

Hannah started twirling her braid. "I'm scared to go by myself, Rachel."

"Oh, all right," said Rachel.

As Rachel hurried home with Hannah, she saw Mrs. Miller leave the drugstore. Rachel imagined the telephone ringing loudly with no one there to take a message.

When they got to their apartment, Rachel said, "Here. You can go in by yourself. And tell Bubbie I'll be home before supper."

As soon as Hannah entered, Rachel turned and went racing back to the drugstore.

"Did anyone else call, Mr. Bloom?" she asked.

"Not in the three and a half minutes since you were gone," said the druggist.

Rachel sat on a stool at the soda fountain. She twirled in circles on the red-padded seat as she waited for the telephone to ring. For a while it was fun. Then she got dizzy and stopped. She traced her finger along a coffee stain on the counter but soon got tired of that. She stared at the telephone. *Ring,* she thought. Customers came and went but the telephone remained silent.

"Why doesn't the telephone ring, Mr. Bloom?" she asked.

"Because no one is calling," he said.

"But someone has to call," said Rachel. "I want to give a message."

"And maybe get a penny?" said Mr. Bloom.

Rachel blushed.

Just then the phone *did* ring. Mr. Bloom spoke into it.

"It's for Herschie at the fish store. Will you get him, Rachel?"

Rachel ran as fast as she could up the street and around the corner. She found Herschie—Mr. Herschel—head down in a fish barrel in front of his store. She cupped her hands and called out to him.

"Mr. Herschel, you have a telephone call."

"*Ach*, it couldn't have come at a worse time," he said.

He popped himself up and a handful of herrings came with him. He shook them off, then rubbed his herring-smelling hands on his apron.

"I suppose it might be important," he said. He yelled into the store to his helper, "Watch the store," and strode away.

Rachel had to run to keep up with him. When they got to the drugstore, she waited impatiently for Mr. Herschel to finish his call. She hoped maybe he would give her more than a penny because she'd had to go so far to get him.

But when he finished, Mr. Herschel left. He didn't give Rachel anything.

"That's how it is with telephone messages—sometimes you get a penny, sometimes you don't," Mr. Bloom said.

"I need that penny, Mr. Bloom!" cried Rachel.

"So who doesn't?" said Mr. Bloom.

Rachel remembered her mother's dream. How many pennies would it take to buy a sewing machine?

"Will you let me stay by the telephone tomorrow, Mr. Bloom?" she asked.

Mr. Bloom shrugged. He went back to his powders.

Rachel waved goodbye. She finally had a job. She hoped there would be more people like Mrs. Miller to take messages to than people like Mr. Herschel. She would keep the pennies she earned safely in her dresser drawer until she could buy her roses.

Rachel held on tightly to her handkerchief and skipped home.

## • seven •

# WORKING HARD

"*Find* a job yet?" Sophie whispered in line at the schoolyard.

"No talking," said the girls' line monitor.

It was time to go in. Rachel whispered, "I did. Tell you about it later."

As the row monitors checked for clean fingernails and handkerchiefs, Rachel daydreamed about her roses. She could almost see them shining on her skirt. It was only the beginning of the day and already she couldn't wait for school to be over.

She felt a tug at her hair.

"Wake up," Izzy whispered. "Where's your hanky?"

Rachel reached into her pocket. It was empty. Where was her handkerchief? She checked her notebook and her desk. It wasn't there. Then she remembered—it was tucked around a penny in her dresser drawer.

"What is the delay, Isadore?" Miss Conway said.

"Um, er, Rachel is looking for her handkerchief, Miss Conway."

"Speak clearly, please. Is Rachel prepared today or is she not?"

"I forgot my handkerchief, Miss Conway," Rachel said.

"I believe I asked Isadore. You are the row monitor?"

"Yes, Miss Conway."

"Then I repeat, is Rachel prepared?"

"No, Miss Conway."

Rachel hung her head as Miss Conway put a demerit in her book.

"You will stay after school, Rachel, and wash the board." Miss Conway looked around the room. "Is anyone else unprepared?" she asked.

Rachel hoped someone else would have to wash the board with her. It would take less time. The room was silent. The board was all hers.

Miss Conway marked papers at her desk after school while Rachel washed the chalky white dust off the front blackboard. She was halfway through when Sophie peeked in.

"Tell Bubbie I'll be late," Rachel whispered.

"This is not a social hour, Miss Berger," said Miss Conway.

Rachel worked as quickly as she could but Miss

Conway was fussy. Even a tiny square of chalk dust meant another trip to the janitor's sink down the hall.

At last Rachel was allowed to leave. She raced home to drop off her books. Homework could wait until later.

When she finally got to the drugstore, all the stools were taken so she stood against the wall by the telephone. She didn't want anyone else to get to it first.

Rachel felt sure there would be a call right away but there wasn't. She shifted from one foot to the other and back again. She tapped her shoe against the wall to a tune she had learned in school. All the waiting made her fidgety.

Izzy came in with his shoeshine box.

"What are you doing here?" he asked.

"What business is it of yours?" she said. She held on to her braids. She wasn't feeling too friendly toward Izzy just then.

"None, I guess."

Izzy went to the counter just as someone got up from the seat. He ordered an egg cream. Rachel watched as Mr. Bloom's assistant poured chocolate syrup into a tall glass. Then he added milk and stirred. When he put in the seltzer, it foamed up to the top of the glass. Rachel could almost taste it. There was nothing better than a cold, fizzy egg cream.

Izzy put two straws into the glass.

"Want to share?" he asked her.

Rachel was ready to forgive him for reporting her but before she could answer, the telephone rang. It was a call for Sophie's house. The egg cream would have to wait.

"Thanks, Izzy, but I have to go," she said, already regretting the lost egg cream.

Rachel ran down the street. She was in such a hurry she tripped and fell. She tore a hole in the elbow of her blouse. Her mother would be mad but she couldn't stop now.

"You're my first call today, Mrs. Gross," she told Sophie's mother. "I came as fast as I could."

"Thank you, Rachel," Sophie's mother said.

"Oh, I hope it's Pa telling us he's coming home," said Sophie. Her father was still selling his wares down south.

"We'll find out soon enough," said Sophie's mother. She was about to leave when Sophie said, "Didn't you forget something, Ma?"

"What do you mean?" asked Mrs. Gross.

"Rachel came all the way from the drugstore to call you."

"Oh."

Mrs. Gross reached into her purse.

"Here is a penny for your trouble, Rachel."

"Thank you," Rachel said. She placed the penny in her pocket. Now she had thirteen cents.

When Mrs. Gross left, Sophie handed Rachel a walnut she had just cracked.

"We're making strudel for the boarders," she said. "They'll never miss one walnut."

Rachel quickly ate the nut.

"I'd better go, Sophie," she said. "I don't want to miss any calls. Thanks for the nut."

Rachel got back to the drugstore just as Mrs. Gross finished with her call. From the look on her face as she rushed out, Rachel knew it wasn't Mr. Gross calling. The telephone rang again right away as if it were trying to help Rachel. There were four messages and three more pennies before Rachel had to go home for supper. That made sixteen cents. She only needed nine more pennies.

Mrs. Golden was standing in the small front room as Rachel entered. She was having a fitting for her dress.

"This is not quite what I had in mind, Mrs. Berger," she said. "I wanted the sleeves to puff at the shoulders and be narrow at the wrists."

"But the styles are changing, Mrs. Golden. Those puffy leg-of-mutton sleeves are dated. Set-in sleeves look so much more elegant."

"Really? I won't pay for anything that isn't in the latest style, you know."

"Rachel," said Mama with a sigh. "Where are your manners? Say hello to Mrs. Golden."

"Hello, Mrs. Golden."

Mrs. Golden looked over at Hannah, who was playing with a top by the front window, then back at Rachel.

"So this is Hannah's big sister."

Rachel gritted her teeth. Was Mrs. Golden comparing them?

"My name is Rachel," she said.

"Well, Rachel, it looks as if your mother needs to make you something better to wear. Ah, but you know the old saying: A shoemaker's children always go barefoot."

Mama's face burned red but she just smiled and bent toward her needle. The metal thimble that protected her finger flashed in the tiny ray of sunshine that came in through the open window.

Rachel tried to hide her torn sleeve. If Mrs. Golden thought Mama wasn't a good dressmaker, she wouldn't recommend Mama to her friends and Mama wouldn't get enough work to buy a sewing machine. Where would Mama's dream be then? Mrs. Golden was Mama's first customer. She was like a fierce wave. Maybe the next wave to come would be gentle. Rachel hoped so.

## · eight ·

# SECRETS

*The* next day Rachel made sure she had her handkerchief. She didn't want Miss Conway to give her another detention.

When she went to the drugstore after school, Mr. Bloom gave her a different job. He paid her a penny to deliver some cough medicine to a man over on the next street. That and the penny she made with one phone message added up to eighteen cents, helping her get closer to the roses. When she closed her eyes, Rachel could see them already shining on her skirt. It made her smile. But there was no time to waste. She felt as if she were in a race with her mother, and her mother was a fast worker.

At supper one night, Mrs. Berger said, "Please get me the buttons, Rachel. I'll be ready to sew them on the skirts tomorrow."

Rachel felt her stomach crunch like the accordion Uncle Duvid played at family gatherings. Except the accordion would go in and out, and Rachel felt as if her stomach was crunched forever. She couldn't tell her mother that she was still saving money to buy the buttons. Mrs. Berger would say she had been foolish for spending so much when she could have settled for the perfectly nice buttons on a card.

"Did you finish Mrs. Golden's dress yet, Mama?" Rachel asked.

"Not yet, but soon."

"When you finish, I'll give you the buttons for both."

"Why not now?" asked her mother.

"Because, because...," Rachel said.

"You didn't lose the nickel I gave you?" asked Mrs. Berger.

"No, Mama. It's just that—"

"Can't you see, Beryl?" said Bubbie. "Our Racheleh has a secret."

Hannah climbed onto Mr. Berger's lap.

"What's a secret, Papa?" she asked.

"A secret, little Hannah, is something you know that no one else knows."

"I want a secret too, Papa," Hannah said.

"She wants everything I have," grumbled Rachel.

"Be a little understanding with your sister," said Papa. "You should feel pleased that she wants to be like you."

Rachel didn't feel one bit pleased.

Papa turned to Hannah.

"So you want a secret."

"Yes, please, Papa," said Hannah.

He bent down and whispered something in Hannah's ear.

Hannah was listening so hard that her eyes closed and her face was all scrunched up. It made everyone laugh.

Rachel was glad Mama had stopped thinking about her. She would have the buttons for her mother in another day or two. When they saw those buttons, they would understand why she had to have them. She would look so grown-up that they'd never ask her to be twins with Hannah again.

Mrs. Golden's dress was almost finished too. The long skirt took up so much room they had to be careful not to step on it.

"What do you think?" Mama asked Rachel.

"It's beautiful, Mama," she said.

Mrs. Berger studied the dress for a minute.

"It still needs something, but I'm not sure what. Maybe a ribbon to trim the collar. It needs a little surprise, a little something unusual to finish it off."

As Rachel tucked Hannah in that night, her sister asked, "What's your secret, Rachel?"

"If I told you it wouldn't be a secret," Rachel said. "Then you would know it too, and you'd tell Mama and Papa."

"No, I wouldn't tell."

"Yes you would."

"Are you collecting pennies for your secret?"

"How do you know about my pennies?" said Rachel.

"I saw you get a penny from Mrs. Miller and I hear you counting them when you think I'm asleep."

Rachel had forgotten that Hannah was with her for that first message at Mr. Bloom's store.

"I'll tell you if you promise to keep it our secret and not tell anyone else."

"I promise," Hannah said.

"What do you promise?"

"I promise not to tell anyone our secret. Not Mama or Papa. Not even Bubbie."

"The secret is..."

"You have to whisper in my ear like Papa did."

Rachel bent down and said softly in Hannah's ear, "I'm saving money to buy special buttons for our skirts."

"Oh, that's a good secret!" said Hannah.

"Now remember, you promised."

"Can I tell Bessie? She won't say anything."

"No. You can't tell Bessie either."

Rachel could just imagine Hannah talking to Bessie under the kitchen table when everyone was around. There would be no secret after that.

"I won't tell anyone, then, Rachel. Not anyone at all."

When Hannah finally fell asleep, Rachel wondered if she should have told. She was sort of glad she had, though.

Having a secret was hard. She wondered if it could be called a secret now that Hannah and Sophie both knew. It seemed like a kind of puzzle she would enjoy figuring out someday, when she didn't have to worry about keeping the secret itself.

## • nine •

# LOST BUTTON

*Bubbie's* feet were acting up when Rachel came home from school. She could hardly stand.

"Why don't you soak them, Bubbie?" said Rachel.

"That's a good idea, Racheleh. But we're out of Epsom salts. Will you go to the drugstore and get some for me?"

"Sure, Bubbie," Rachel said. She was going there anyway. She had the cloth purse with eighteen cents inside. She didn't want Hannah looking into her stuff. Besides, she needed seven more pennies. Maybe she would get lucky and have lots of telephone calls. Then she would go straight to see Mr. Solomon.

"Tell Mr. Bloom to put it on my account."

"Okay."

"And take Hannah with you."

The pain on Bubbie's face stopped any argument. Rachel took Hannah's hand and quietly closed the door.

"Are you getting the buttons, Rachel?" Hannah whispered on the way. Hannah loved whispering.

"Not yet," Rachel whispered back.

"I can help," Hannah whispered.

"You're too little to help," whispered Rachel.

"Mama let me help with her secret," Hannah whispered.

"What secret?" said Rachel, not whispering at all.

"I can't tell. When I went to get a drink last night I saw Mama working on something special. She made me promise just like you did."

Hannah skipped down the street. Rachel was so surprised she couldn't move. Mama had a secret too? One she'd only told to Hannah?

Rachel took a deep breath. She would have to find out about Mama's secret later. There was too much to do right now. She chased after Hannah and they entered the drugstore together.

Rachel asked for the Epsom salts. As she waited for the package, she looked at the silent telephone. Would it ring today? This was the last chance she had to get the buttons. The dress was finished. Her mother would need the buttons, but they were still in Mr. Solomon's store. And Mr. Solomon had said he would only hold them until the holiday. Then they would go back into the bin, where someone else would probably buy them. Tomorrow night was the start of Rosh Hashanah.

"Here you go, girls," Mr. Bloom said. "Tell your grandmother I hope her feet are better."

"Thank you, Mr. Bloom," they said.

As they left the store, the phone rang. What should Rachel do? Walk Hannah home and miss the call or run back now? Maybe she could get her roses after all. The phone rang again. It was as if the jangling bell were calling to her. It needed her as much as she needed it.

Rachel shoved the package into Hannah's hands.

"Here, Hannah. You take this to Bubbie. I'll watch you go up the street."

"But Rachel..."

"Go. Go on. Hurry."

Hannah raced up the block to their house. Before she even started up the stoop, Rachel rushed back into the drugstore.

"Rachel, there's a call for Mr. Carnovitz. Will you please get him? I saw him go down to the delicatessen."

Mr. Carnovitz was at the counter ordering some corned beef when a panting Rachel gave him the message.

"A telephone call? For me? I never had a telephone call before," said Mr. Carnovitz.

He ran out of the delicatessen, leaving his food on the counter, and headed straight to the drugstore.

It didn't even matter that he hadn't given Rachel a penny. One penny wouldn't have been enough. She still needed seven cents. But he had to come back for his packages. Maybe he would give her a penny then. Rachel decided to wait.

Simcha was behind the counter helping her mother.

"Hi, Rachel," she said. "Can you play? Mother said I can take a few minutes off."

"Sure."

They sat on two orange crates in front of the store. Simcha had a piece of string, so they played cat's cradle. Rachel usually liked making the string forms with her fingers, but today her heart wasn't in it. It was taking Mr. Carnovitz too long.

"I'd better go," Rachel said.

There was no way she would be able to get the roses now. Even if Mr. Carnovitz gave her a penny she wouldn't have time to get all the money she'd need. She would take some of her money and buy ordinary, everyday, nothing-special buttons for the skirts.

Just then Mr. Carnovitz came charging into the store.

"What a telephone call!" he said. "I forget everything, even the groceries. That was my brother. He's here! I have waited so long for him to come to this country!"

Mr. Carnovitz was so excited he was dancing in circles right in front of everyone.

"Thank you, thank you," he said as he pressed something into Rachel's hand. "Here. Take this for the wonderful message you have brought me!"

Mr. Carnovitz wasn't nearly as excited as Rachel. He'd given her a dime! Ten cents! She had twenty-eight cents, three more than she needed. She could hardly believe it. Now she could have her roses and help her mother even more! She ran to Sophie's house first.

"I did it, Sophie, I did it! Let's get the buttons!"

Sophie put aside her homework, called out to her mother, and flew with Rachel down the stairs.

Rachel watched Mr. Solomon count the money she gave him. She was afraid that maybe she had counted wrong. Or maybe she had lost some on the way over.

But Mr. Solomon smiled.

"It's all here," he said.

He reached under the counter and took out the envelope he had been saving for her. "The buttons are yours," he said.

Rachel's hands shook as she took the envelope from Mr. Solomon.

"Thank you," she said as calmly as she could, but she

wasn't really feeling very calm inside. A bubbling pot of Mama's stew was more like how she felt.

As soon as they stepped out of the store, Rachel had her hand inside the envelope.

"Let's see, let's see," said Sophie.

Three glass balls stared up at them from Rachel's palm.

"Look how they sparkle, Sophie," said Rachel.

She held one up so the light could shine through it. All of a sudden, they heard someone yell, "Grab him!"

Before they could move, Izzy's little brother, Jacob, came charging toward them with Izzy pointing and waving like a madman half a step behind.

"Can't catch me, Izzy!" Jacob dodged around the girls, but Izzy bumped into them. He, Sophie, and Rachel fell to the ground. The rose buttons flew out of Rachel's hand.

"Look what you made me do, Izzy!" she yelled.

"Why didn't you stop him?" Izzy yelled back. He scrambled to his feet. "I've got to get my brother!" he called over his shoulder as he sped off.

"Help me find them, Sophie!" Rachel cried as she got up to look for the buttons.

Sophie found one in front of Mr. Solomon's store. Rachel found one in a dirty crack a few feet away. But the third button was nowhere to be seen. They looked in

every crack and behind every pushcart wheel. The last button had disappeared.

"Maybe Mr. Solomon has another one," said Sophie.

"He said these were the only three he had," Rachel said. "Besides, my mother needs the buttons now."

Sophie picked up the envelope and took out the button card that was still inside.

"The buttons on the card are pretty," she said.

"Yes, but they aren't my roses!" cried Rachel. Tears poured down her face as she headed home.

"I'll never speak to that Izzy again as long as I live!"

# ten

# LOST HANNAH

*Rachel* stomped up the tenement stairs. First her mother had quit her job. Now one of the buttons she had saved so hard to buy was lost, so she would have to wear the same skirt as Hannah. Everything was going wrong.

"Ah, Racheleh," Bubbie said as soon as she walked in. "I've been waiting. Give me the Epsom salts before my feet swell to the size of pickle barrels."

"Didn't Hannah give you the package from the drugstore?" Rachel asked.

That Hannah! She couldn't be trusted to do anything right.

"Hannah is with you. Why should she be carrying the package?"

"But Hannah isn't with me, Bubbie. I sent her home long ago."

Everything stopped in the room. Bubbie stopped talking. Mrs. Berger stopped sewing. Rachel stopped breathing.

Where was Hannah?

"Why isn't she with you?" asked Mrs. Berger. "Where is she, Rachel?"

"I don't know, Mama. I watched while she went to the steps. I thought she would go right into the house."

*Where would she go?* Rachel thought.

"You left her by herself?" yelled Mrs. Berger.

Mrs. Berger pushed aside the hem she was working on. Mrs. Golden was due to pick up her dress in the morning and there were still a few last details to finish. With Hannah missing, Mrs. Golden's dress would have to wait.

"We have to find her. Now!" said Rachel's mother. "The sun is setting. She won't know her way home in the dark."

Mrs. Berger rushed off to knock on the neighbors' doors. Maybe one of them had seen Hannah.

Rachel ran to her school. Hannah was always saying she couldn't wait to go there. But the yard was empty and the doors were shut tight.

When Rachel returned home, her mother was just coming up the stairs. Hannah was not with her. Where could they look now? Mrs. Berger went to look in the stores down the street.

"Phil, have you seen Hannah?" Rachel asked as Phil was packing up his pushcart. "She's lost. No one knows where she is."

"I saw her this afternoon," said Phil. "She was going toward Delancey Street. She had a package. I thought she was taking it somewhere."

*She should have been taking it to Bubbie,* thought Rachel. *Why was she going to Delancey Street?* Of all places to get lost, Hannah had picked the biggest, busiest, most crowded street. How would Rachel ever find her?

As she ran, Rachel imagined terrible things. She imagined Hannah trampled by a horse. She imagined her sister wandering in a strange part of the city and crying out for her. She ran faster.

Delancey Street was so big, Rachel didn't know where to start looking. She dashed into the first store, where a man was fitting a customer for a hat.

"Did you see a little girl all by herself?" she asked him.

"No, no little girl," he said.

Rachel went to the next store and the next and the next. No one had seen Hannah. The long street was filled with stores. Surely someone had seen her sister. Rachel wouldn't go home until she'd searched all the stores.

It was getting late. Rachel was getting scared. What if Hannah tried to cross the street by herself? What if Rachel couldn't find her? No, Rachel would keep looking, even if it took all night and the next day. She went into a candy store and asked about Hannah for what seemed the hundredth time. She was ready to walk out, even before the clerk answered, and go on to the next store.

"A little girl? All alone? Do you mean the one sitting in the back by the telephone?"

There, on the dusty floor, sat Hannah. She was twirling her tangled braid. Her little foot kept tapping against the wall as if she was impatient for something. For a second, Rachel remembered herself sitting by Mr. Bloom's telephone in the very same way.

"Hannah! What are you doing here?"

"I'm helping, Rachel. I'm waiting for the telephone to ring so I can get a penny to give to you." She stood up and whispered in Rachel's ear. "Then you can get the buttons."

"Oh, Hannah. You had us all so worried. Everyone is out looking for you."

"No one called, Rachel. I went to all the stores until I found a telephone but it didn't ring."

Rachel thought of the first wave Bubbie had told her about. Hannah had followed her like the waves follow each other to the shore. Being a first wave was really an important job, and a big responsibility too.

"It doesn't matter, Hannah," said Rachel. She grabbed the bag of Epsom salts and said, "Come. Let's go home."

Izzy caught up with them on their way.

"I didn't mean to knock you down, Rachel," he said. "I was supposed to watch my brother while my mother was in the pickle store but he ran away. I had to get him before she finished shopping." Izzy took a deep breath and then said, "Sometimes being a big brother isn't easy."

Rachel realized that Izzy was a first wave too. He had just been doing his job, getting his runaway brother back.

Izzy looked down at his shoes.

"Sophie told me about your button. I looked for it after I brought my brother back to the store."

"You did?" asked Rachel. "Did you find it?"

"Not right away," he said. "I looked under every tree, in the cement cracks, in the gutter and...here."

He reached into his pocket and handed something to Rachel.

"My button!" Rachel shrieked.

"It was stuck between the bricks by Mr. Solomon's store. The red color blended in with the bricks."

Izzy raised his hand as if to tug Rachel's braid but stopped.

"Bye, Rachel," he said, and ran home.

Rachel looked at the button in her hand. Something felt different. She'd worked so hard to buy the buttons, but they didn't seem so important anymore. She'd almost lost Hannah because she wanted them so much.

She led Hannah upstairs.

Papa was home now. He was getting ready to join the search. They all shouted when they saw Hannah. Everyone talked at once.

"You're home!"

"Thank goodness."

"We were so worried."

"Where were you?"

Hannah looked at Rachel. Then she said, "I took a walk."

"Don't ever do that again, Hannah!" scolded Mama before she grabbed Hannah into a big hug.

Rachel was glad that Mama didn't seem mad anymore.

Supper was hurried that night. There was so much work to do. Hannah wanted to stay up late but she was too tired. She fell asleep at the table. Papa carried her to bed. She stirred as Rachel tucked her in.

"Rachel?"

"Shh. Go back to sleep, Hannah."

"I didn't tell the secret, Rachel."

"I know. Only babies tell secrets. You're not a baby."

Hannah smiled a sleepy smile.

"Tell me another secret," said Hannah.

Rachel bent down and whispered, "Rosh Hashanah starts tomorrow night."

"I won't tell," Hannah said as she drifted off to sleep.

As Rachel watched Hannah sleeping so peacefully, she suddenly knew what she wanted to do with the buttons.

# eleven

# RACHEL'S ROSES

"*It's* time for the buttons, Rachel," said Mrs. Berger after Hannah had gone to bed.

Rachel reached into her pocket. She felt the roses that she'd worked so hard to get. But what she pulled out instead was the polka-dot button card. It felt so different in her hand now, almost exciting.

More than anything, after what Hannah had done, Rachel wanted to share the same buttons with her sister. This Rosh Hashanah, she and Hannah would be like two waves coming ashore at the same time.

She handed the button card to Mama.

"Those are pretty, but I thought you were going to get different buttons," her mother said.

Rachel just smiled and said, "May I help sew them on?"

"Yes," Mama said.

She grinned as she gave Rachel some thread and handed her the skirts.

Rachel's mouth dropped open.

"Mama! Our old skirts look so different!" she said. Rachel's skirt had a row of red plaid pleats on the bottom. Hannah's skirt had a red plaid ruffle on the bottom!

"Do you like your skirt?" Mama asked.

Rachel hugged her skirt and said, "I love it!" She bet that Hannah would love her skirt too.

So that was Mama's secret. She had made their old skirts look new—and special! Rachel and Hannah wouldn't be twins after all.

Mrs. Berger showed Rachel where to place the buttons so they would line up with the buttonholes. Then they both set to work. Her mother sewed faster but Rachel didn't care. She worked slowly so she would do a good job.

As she sewed, she thought of Hannah getting lost just so she could get a penny to give to Rachel. When Rachel had found her, Hannah was sitting in the dust. Her hair was in a tangle. She was tugging on it so she wouldn't be afraid. The clothes Bubbie had so carefully washed and ironed looked ragged.

At that moment Rachel *knew*—she didn't have to wait for someday anymore. She understood what Bubbie meant about silk and rags. Something nice inside was more important than what was on the outside. New skirts were nice to have but a sister like Hannah was silk in the cupboard.

"Very good," said Mama when Rachel showed her the finished work. "Soon you'll be ready to be an assistant dressmaker."

Mama finished sewing the hem and laid out Mrs. Golden's dress on the table.

Rachel took one of the glass buttons she had hidden in her pocket and held it against her skirt. The button was just perfect for it, as she knew it would be, but the rose would be even better somewhere else.

"Mama," she said. "I know what Mrs. Golden's dress needs."

She got the other buttons and set them in a row down the front of Mrs. Golden's dress. They looked as if they had always been there.

"Rachel. That's it!" said Mrs. Berger. "Where did you get these?"

"I earned the money by delivering phone messages, Mama. Then I bargained with Mr. Solomon for them," said Rachel, "and he gave me the polka dots too."

"But you decided to use the same buttons as Hannah. What a good sister you are."

Mama hugged Rachel. "And what a good daughter."

Mama got back to work. She was as excited as she had been on the day she left Mr. Lempkin to become a dressmaker. Mama's dream was shining in her eyes.

"This is just right!" Mama said when she had finished. "I think Mrs. Golden will be pleased."

❖ ❖ ❖

In the early morning, everyone was busy. Bubbie shuffled off to the fish store for some of Mr. Herschel's herrings.

Papa said he would bring home some new white candles after work.

"Go to Phil's pushcart and buy an apple," Mama said as she handed Rachel a coin. "And then take this jar and ask Mrs. Gross if we can borrow a little bit of honey."

Downstairs, the street was more crowded than usual. Rachel had to squeeze her way between people just to get to the fruit cart.

She bought the best apple Phil had. Rachel loved dipping apples in honey. Bubbie said it was a wish for a sweet year.

With apple in hand, Rachel went to Sophie's house. Sophie filled half the jar with honey from the bottle on the shelf and handed it back to Rachel. Sophie's apartment was steamy with the smells of cooking fish and potato soup.

Mrs. Golden was already in the apartment when Rachel returned. She had on the dress. Would she like it? She turned one way, then the other. She tugged at this and pulled at that. She sat down and stood up. Mrs. Berger stood there watching.

Finally, Mrs. Golden said, "I like it, Mrs. Berger. You were right about the sleeves. And these beautiful roses add just the right touch. I will tell my friends."

As Mrs. Golden was changing into her street clothes, Rachel felt the dream whirling inside her mother.

"I have something for you, Mama," she said.

Rachel reached inside her pocket and took out her

handkerchief. Inside were the three extra pennies she had earned. "This is to help with your dream."

Mama opened her mouth to say something but nothing came out. Her eyes glowed with tears. Mrs. Berger hugged Rachel.

"Come right home from school," Mama said softly.

"I will."

Rachel put her handkerchief back in her pocket. She was not going to stay after school again, not today.

❖ ❖ ❖

The day seemed to move like a turtle with no place to go. When school was finally over, Rachel sped home to help get ready for the holiday. As the sun began to go down, she took Hannah into their room and announced to the rest of the family, "Don't come in, anyone."

"I wonder what is happening in there," said Mrs. Berger.

"A secret is happening," said Bubbie.

Papa came home with the candles. They weren't so new and they weren't so white.

"I found them in the street vendor's basket," he said. "He needed the money more than we needed them new."

"They're lovely, Samuel," said Mrs. Berger.

"Look at us, Mama! Look, Papa! Look, Bubbie!" called Hannah from the bedroom doorway.

"Well, come out here so we can see you," Papa said.

Hannah skipped into the kitchen. Rachel came in behind her.

Hannah's hair was in neat braids, just like Rachel's. At the end of the braids were tiny pink ribbons, just like Rachel wore. And they both had on the new red plaid skirts that Mama had made, with the same polka-dot buttons.

"We're twins!" said Hannah.

Mrs. Berger looked at her daughters.

"You are almost like Rachel," said Mama. "But you still have some growing to do before you are as grown-up as your sister."

"I am grown-up. I can keep a secret," said Hannah. "I won't tell anyone that today is Rosh Hashanah!"

Everyone laughed.

"We know it already," said Bubbie.

"Did Rachel tell you?" asked Hannah.

"No," Bubbie said. "This is a secret for everyone. When the town clock chimes, we all hear our own song."

Rachel didn't really understand what Bubbie meant, but she didn't ask her to explain. She would figure it out.

"It's time for apples and honey," said Mrs. Berger.

They all took an apple slice and dipped it into the sticky honey.

"This is going to be a sweet year," said Papa.

"No, Papa," said Rachel, smiling at Bubbie. Then she dipped another slice of apple into the honey and handed it to Hannah. "This is going to be a silk year."

"I don't understand," Papa said.

"Someday you'll know," said Rachel.

# AUTHOR'S NOTE

Rosh Hashanah, the Jewish New Year that comes around the beginning of the Fall season, always felt special for me when I was growing up. As sunset turned into night, I was eager to start the holiday with my first taste of apples and honey. It was a wish for the coming year to be sweet and good.

In the morning, getting dressed, I always wanted to wear something new to honor the occasion. In the book, Rachel hoped that Mama would make her a new skirt for the holiday, but even though her skirt wasn't brand new, Mama made it look like new with pretty red pleats on the bottom. I often received my older cousin's outgrown clothes and would choose a dress or a scarf, a bracelet or a handkerchief that she gave me to wear. Even though they were used, they were new to me and I loved wearing what she gave me!

My family and I would walk to services at the synagogue a few blocks away. Even before we went inside,

I could hear the sound of the prayers as they rang out onto the street. I would feel them in my heart.

Rosh Hashanah is a sacred time, a time to ask for forgiveness, to think about how to be a better person and make the world a better place. I would plan to be more helpful to my mother, to work harder at school, and to be nicer to my sister. I knew that Rosh Hashanah would be over soon, but I hoped I would remember to keep my plans through the whole year. And when the holiday returned the next year, I knew it would feel special again.